Planting a Rainbow

Written and illustrated by
Lois Ehlert

Houghton Mifflin Harcourt

Boston New York

DEDICATED TO SHIRLEY AND DICK

For information about permission to reproduce
selections from this book, please write to
Permissions, Houghton Mifflin Harcourt
Publishing Company 215 Park
Avenue South NY NY 10003.

www.hmhco.com

Library of Congress Cataloging-in-Publication Data
Ehlert, Lois.
Planting a rainbow.
Summary: A mother and child plant a rainbow of
flowers in the family garden.
ISBN 978-0-15-262609-9
ISBN 978-0-15-262610-5 pb
ISBN 978-0-15-262611-2 oversize pb
[1. Gardening—Fiction.   2. Flowers—Fiction.
3. Mother and child—Fiction.]
I. Title.
PZ7.E3225P1   1988   [E]   87-8528

SCP   47 46 45 44 43 42 41
4500517376

Printed in China

Every year Mom and
I plant a rainbow

In the fall we buy some bulbs

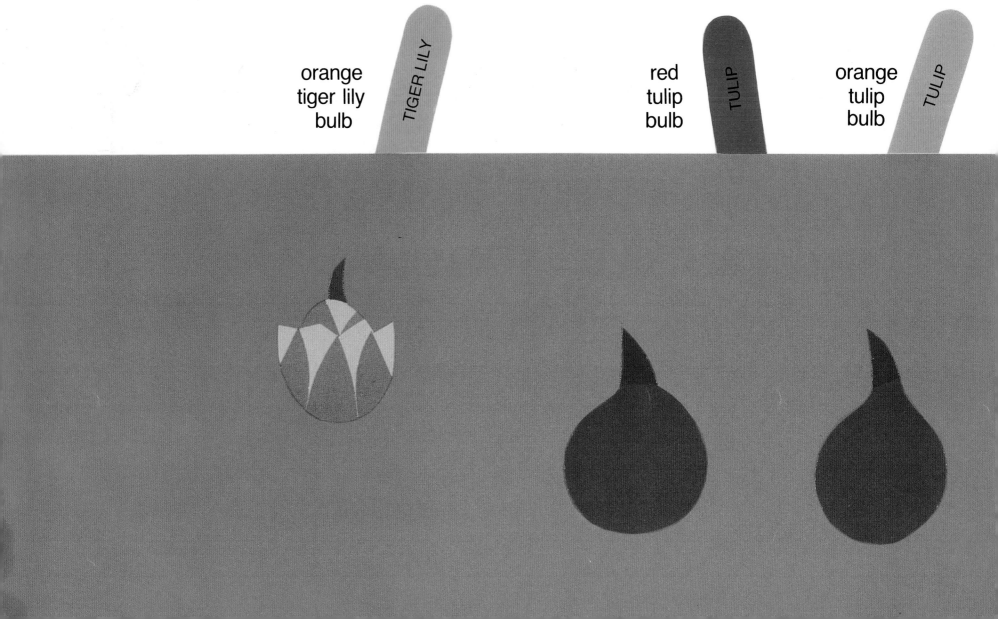

orange
tiger lily
bulb

TIGER LILY

red
tulip
bulb

TULIP

orange
tulip
bulb

TULIP

and plant them in the ground.

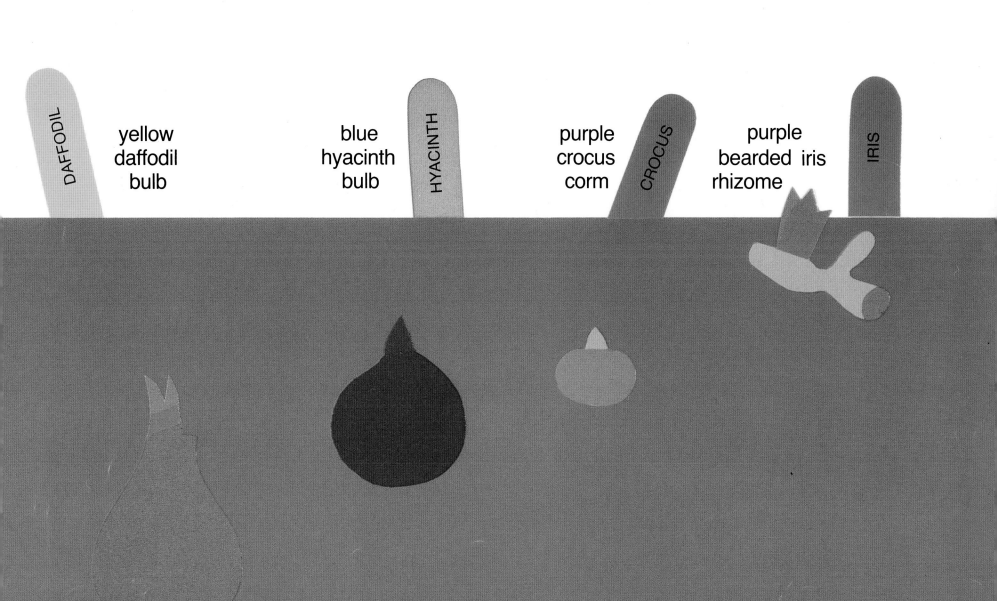

DAFFODIL

yellow
daffodil
bulb

blue
hyacinth
bulb

HYACINTH

purple
crocus
corm

CROCUS

purple
bearded iris
rhizome

IRIS

We order seeds from catalogs and

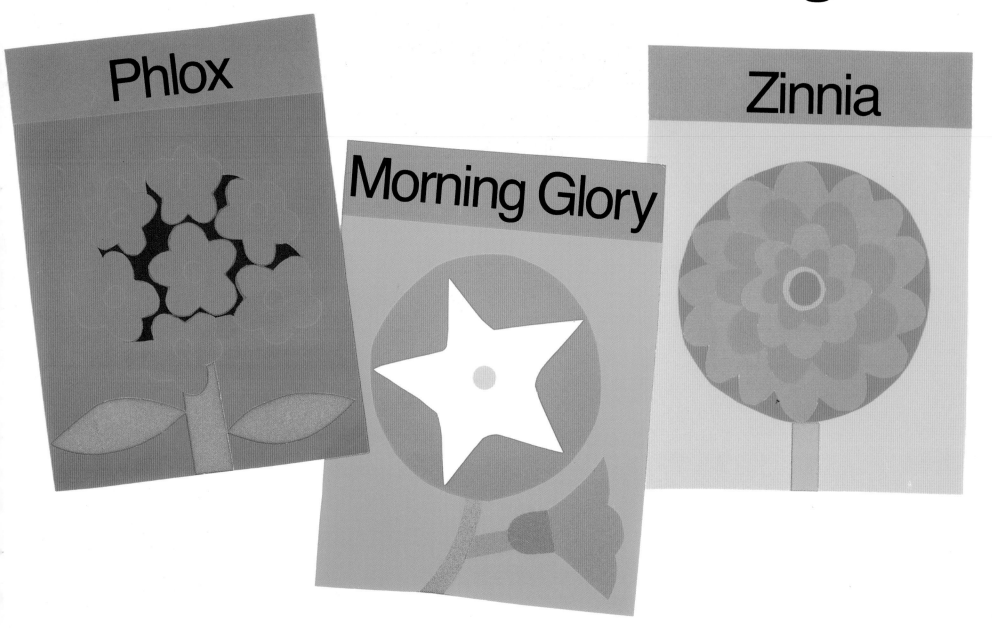

Phlox

Morning Glory

Zinnia

wait all winter long

Marigold

Cornflower

Aster

Daisy

for spring to warm the soil and sprout the bulbs.

TULIP

TULIP

DAFFODIL

HYACINTH

CROCUS

TULIP

TULIP

DAFFODIL

HYACINTH

CROCUS

Then it's time to go to the garden center to select some seedlings.

We sow the seeds and set out the

plants in soil,

and watch the

TIGER LILY

DAISY

PHLOX

ASTER

CARNATION

ROSE

VIOLET

DELPHINIUM

rainbow grow,

and grow,

and grow.

carnations

tulips

zinnia

and
orange
flowers,

tulip

We have some red flowers

rose

and
some
yellow
blooms.

daisy

marigold

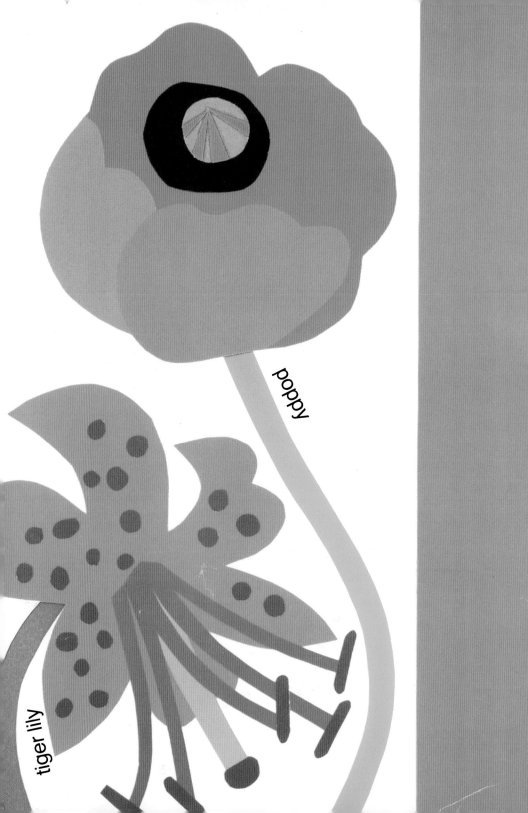

poppy

tiger lily

We grow something green

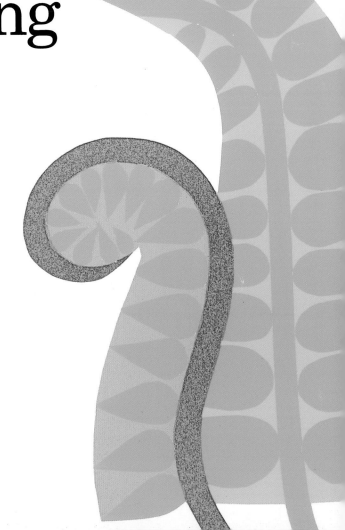

daffodils

ferns

and
some blue
flowers,

morning
glories

delphinium

hyacinth

cornflowers

and some
purple
flowers,
too.

phlox

crocus

iris

violets

asters

pansy

All summer long
we pick them
and bring them home.

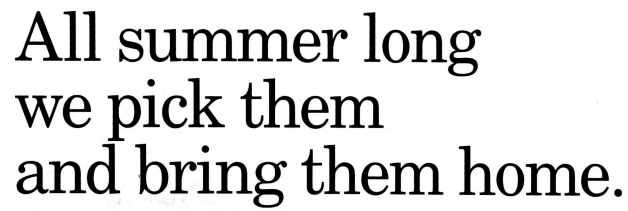

And when summer is over, we know we can grow our rainbow again next year.